EARLY BIRD STORIES

My Family Celebrates
HANUKKAH

Lisa Bullard

Illustrated by Constanza Basaluzzo

LERNER PUBLICATIONS ◆ MINNEAPOLIS

NOTE TO EDUCATORS

Find text recall questions at the end of each chapter. Critical-thinking and text feature questions are available on page 23. These help young readers learn to think critically about the topic by using the text, text features, and illustrations.

Lerner Publications Company
A division of Lerner Publishing Group, Inc.
241 First Avenue North
Minneapolis, MN 55401 USA

For reading levels and more information, look up this title at www.lernerbooks.com.

Photos on p. 22 used with permission of: Silver Spiral Arts/Shutterstock.com (menorah); Mordechai Meiri/Shutterstock.com (dreidels); Derek Hatfield/Shutterstock.com (coins).

Main body text set in Billy Infant 22/28.
Typeface provided by SparkyType.

Library of Congress Cataloging-in-Publication Data

Names: Bullard, Lisa, author. | Basaluzzo, Constanza, illustrator.
Title: My family celebrates Hanukkah / Lisa Bullard ; illustrated by Constanza Basaluzzo.
Description: Minneapolis, MN : Lerner Publications, [2019] | Series: Holiday time (Early bird stories TM) | Includes bibliographical references and index.
Identifiers: LCCN 2017049349 (print) | LCCN 2017056391 (ebook) | ISBN 9781541524996 (eb pdf) | ISBN 9781541520066 (lb : alk. paper) | ISBN 9781541527416 (pb : alk. paper)
Subjects: LCSH: Hanukkah—Juvenile literature.
Classification: LCC BM695.H3 (ebook) | LCC BM695.H3 B854 2019 (print) | DDC 296.4/35—dc23

LC record available at https://lccn.loc.gov/2017049349

Manufactured in the United States of America
1-44342-34588-1/15/2018

TABLE OF CONTENTS

CHAPTER 1
THE HANUKKAH STORY

Hi, I'm Caleb! This dreidel is part of a fun Hanukkah game!

Hanukkah is a Jewish holiday. It starts tonight, so I'm practicing.

5

I practice while my dad tells me the Hanukkah story.

More than two thousand years ago, a Greek king named Antiochus IV made it against the law to practice the Jewish religion. He took over the Jewish Temple in Jerusalem.

7

But some Jewish people fought back.

They beat the king's army. They took back their temple. They were free to practice their religion!

Who made it against the law to practice the Jewish religion?

CHAPTER 2

A MIRACLE HAPPENED

The Jewish people cleaned the temple so they could use it again. They lit the temple's oil lamp. But there was only enough oil to light the lamp for one day.

Then a miracle happened. The oil lasted for eight days! That's why we celebrate eight days of Hanukkah.

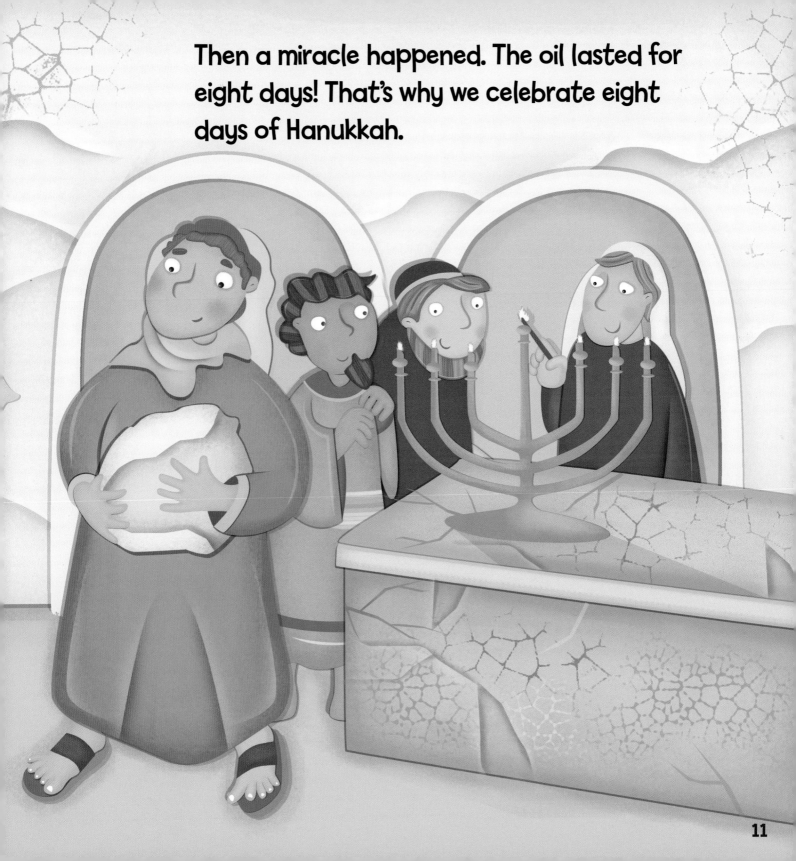

My dreidel has Hebrew letters on it. They stand for "A great miracle happened there."

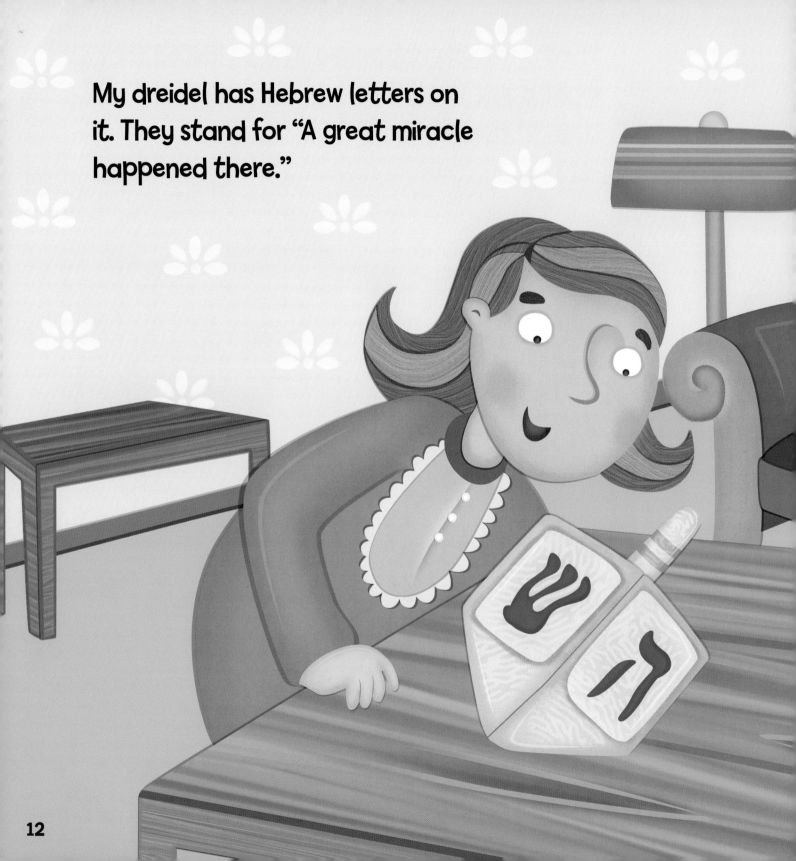

CHAPTER 3

LIGHTING THE CANDLES

Relatives come over to celebrate. When the sun sets, we light the first candle on the menorah.

Each night of Hanukkah, we'll add another candle.

The kids get Hanukkah gelt! That's money. Some of the coins are chocolate. Some are real.

I'll share some of mine with people who need it more.

We eat latkes. Those are potato pancakes. Mom fries them in oil. The oil reminds us of the Hanukkah miracle.

What is gelt?

19

CHAPTER 4

DREIDEL TIME

It's dreidel time! I win a pile of chocolate coins.

There are seven more nights of Hanukkah. We'll celebrate with seven more nights of dreidel!

What does Caleb win?

LEARN ABOUT HOLIDAYS

Hanukkah usually takes place in December.

Hanukkah began in the city of Jerusalem. It is in the country now called Israel. Today, Jewish people around the world celebrate Hanukkah.

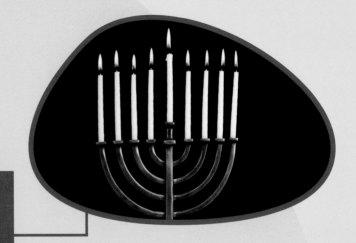

Hanukkah is also called the Festival of Lights. People light the menorah each night. Families often put their menorah in a window.

People use small items like coins or chocolate as game pieces in dreidel. Players take turns spinning. The Hebrew letter that lands up tells what happens next. The player to get all the pieces is the winner.

Many children get gifts or money for Hanukkah. Some share these gifts with others. Sharing is part of the Jewish religion.

THINK ABOUT HOLIDAYS: CRITICAL-THINKING AND TEXT FEATURE QUESTIONS

Why do Jewish families celebrate Hanukkah?

Why do kids share their Hanukkah gifts?

Who wrote this book?

Where can you find the table of contents in this book?

GLOSSARY

dreidel: a four-sided spinning top

menorah: a special candleholder used in the Jewish religion

miracle: an incredible or unusual event, thing, or accomplishment

religion: a set of beliefs in a god or gods

temple: a building where the Jewish religion is practiced

TO LEARN MORE

BOOKS
Nelson, Robin. *Crayola Hanukkah Colors*. Minneapolis: Lerner Publications, 2019. Learn more about the colors of Hanukkah in this book.

Simon, Richard, and Tonya Simon. *Oskar and the Eight Blessings*. New York: Roaring Brook, 2015. Join Oskar as he travels to New York City on the eighth night of Hanukkah.

WEBSITE
Chanukah
http://www.chabad.org/kids/article_cdo/aid/354748/jewish/Chanukah.htm
Find videos, stories, songs, and games for Hanukkah at this website.

INDEX